The Bear Went Over the Mountain

The Bear Went Over the Mountain

as told and illustrated by
Iza Trapani

Sky Pony Press
New York

To Anne, Denis, Damian, and Virginio, with love, Iza

Sky Pony Press books may be purchased in bulk at special discounts for sales promotion, corporate gifts, fund-raising, or educational purposes. Special editions can also be created to specifications. For details, contact the Special Sales Department, Sky Pony Press, 307 West 36th Street, 11th Floor, New York, NY 10018 or info@skyhorsepublishing.com.

Sky Pony Press® is a registered trademark of Skyhorse Publishing, Inc.®, a Delaware corporation.

Visit our website at www.skyponypress.com.

10 9 8 7 6 5 4 3 2 1

Manufactured in China, January 2012
This product conforms to CPSIA 2008

Library of Congress Cataloging-in-Publication Data

Trapani, Iza.
The bear went over the mountain / as told and illustrated by Iza Trapani.
    p. cm.
Summary: In this expanded version of the traditional song, a bear goes exploring near his home in the mountains, using all five senses throughout the four seasons.
  ISBN 978-1-61608-510-0 (hardcover : alk. paper)
  1. Children's songs--Texts. [1. Songs. 2. Bears--Songs and music. 3. Nature--Songs and music. 4. Senses and sensation--Songs and music. 5. Seasons--Songs and music.] .I. Title.
  PZ8.3.T686Be 2012
  782.42--dc23
  [E]
            2011044098

Editors: Jean Reynolds and Julie Matysik
Designer: Brian Peterson
Managing Editor: Abigail Gehring

The bear went over the mountain,
The bear went over the mountain,
The bear went over the mountain
To see what he could see.

He saw a dragonfly,
A bluebird flitting by,
Three fuzzy rabbits skipping,
Five happy ducklings dipping,

One mama duck come nipping
To chase him up a tree!

The bear went over the mountain,
The bear went over the mountain,
The bear went over the mountain
To hear what he could hear.

He heard a cricket chirp,
A woodchuck sip and slurp,
The hum of froggies peeping,
The burst of birdies cheeping,

The swish of something creeping
And hissing in his ear!

The bear went over the mountain,
The bear went over the mountain,
The bear went over the mountain
To smell what he could smell.

He smelled the spicy pines,
Sweet honeysuckle vines,
The minty grasses swaying,
The moldy leaves decaying,

A skunk beside him spraying—
It's time to say farewell!

The bear went over the mountain,
The bear went over the mountain,
The bear went over the mountain
To touch what he could touch.

He touched a soggy log,
A wet and warty frog,
A minnow, slick and shiny,
A blossom, soft and tiny,

A porcupine, all spiny—
He did not like it much!

The bear went over the mountain,
The bear went over the mountain,
The bear went over the mountain
To taste what he could taste.

He tasted tangy shrubs,
Delicious, juicy grubs,
A beechnut, tough and chewy,
Some berries, tart and dewy,

And honey, sweet and gooey,
But then away he raced!

The bear went over the mountain,
The bear went over the mountain,
The bear went over the mountain
To go back home again.

Back down the other side,
He plodded, satisfied.
His spirits were just soaring
From all of his exploring,

And now the bear is snoring,
Snugly in his den.

The bear went o - ver the moun - tain, the bear went o - ver the

moun - tain, the bear went o - ver the moun - tain to see what he could

see. He saw a dra - gon fly, a blue - bird flit - ting

by, three fuz - zy ra - bbits skip - ping, five ha - ppy duck - lings

dip - ping, one ma - ma du - ck come nip - ping to chase him up a

tree.

2. The bear went over the mountain,

The bear went over the mountain,

The bear went over the mountain

To hear what he could hear.

He heard a cricket chirp,
A woodchuck sip and slurp,
The hum of froggies peeping,
The burst of birdies cheeping,
The swish of something creeping
And hissing in his ear!

3. The bear went over the mountain,

The bear went over the mountain,

The bear went over the mountain

To smell what he could smell.

He smelled the spicy pines,
Sweet honeysuckle vines,
The minty grasses swaying,
The moldy leaves decaying,
A skunk beside him spraying—
It's time to say farewell!

4. The bear went over the mountain,

The bear went over the mountain,

The bear went over the mountain

To touch what he could touch.

He touched a soggy log,
A wet and warty frog,
A minnow, slick and shiny,
A blossom, soft and tiny,
A porcupine, all spiny—
He did not like it much!

5. The bear went over the mountain,

The bear went over the mountain,

The bear went over the mountain

To taste what he could taste.

He tasted tangy shrubs,
Delicious, juicy grubs,
A beechnut, tough and chewy,
Some berries, tart and dewy,
And honey, sweet and gooey,
But then away he raced!

6. The bear went over the mountain,

The bear went over the mountain,

The bear went over the mountain

To go back home again.

Back down the other side,
He plodded, satisfied.
His spirits were just soaring
From all of his exploring,
And now the bear is snoring,
Snugly in his den.